SNAP-HAPPY ANNIE

June Crebbin

Illustrated by Emily Bolam

PUFFIN BOOKS

SNAP-HAPPY ANNIE

For the Telford boys,
Callum, Edward and James

J.C.

PUFFIN BOOKS

Published by the Penguin Group
Penguin Books Ltd, 27 Wrights Lane, London W8 5TZ, England
Penguin Putnam Inc., 375 Hudson Street, New York, New York 10014, USA
Penguin Books Australia Ltd, Ringwood, Victoria, Australia
Penguin Books Canada Ltd, 10 Alcorn Avenue, Toronto, Ontario, Canada M4V 3B2
Penguin Books (NZ) Ltd, Private Bag 102902, NSMC, Auckland, New Zealand

Penguin Books Ltd, Registered Offices: Harmondsworth, Middlesex, England

On the World Wide Web at: www.penguin.com

First published by Viking 1999
Published in Puffin Books 2000
1 3 5 7 9 10 8 6 4 2

Text copyright © June Crebbin, 1999
Illustrations copyright © Emily Bolam, 1999
All rights reserved

The moral right of the author and illustrator has been asserted

Made and printed in Italy by Printer Trento Srl

British Library Cataloguing in Publication Data
A CIP catalogue record for this book is available from the British Library

ISBN 0–140–56467–5

Down by the banks of a river lived a crocodile called Annie.
One day she went to Monkey's happy-birthday party.
"Now just behave," said her mother. "And don't go
SNIP-SNAPPING all over the place. It's not nice."

Annie looked around. There were lots of things to play with. Monkey was playing with a new bouncy ball.

"I want that ball," said Annie. "Give it to me."

"No," said Monkey.

Annie opened her mouth with all her teeth sharp as knives.
SNIP - SNAP! went Annie's teeth, dangerously close to
Monkey's tail.
Monkey dropped the ball. She didn't want to lose her tail.

Annie liked playing with the
ball. She juggled it on her nose.
She batted it up and down.
She threw it in the air.

It stuck in a tree.
Annie looked round. Parrot was having a swing.

"I want a swing," said Annie. "Get off that swing."
"No," said Parrot.

Annie opened her mouth with all her teeth sharp as scissors.
SNIP - SNAP! went Annie's teeth, dangerously close to Parrot's wing.

Parrot flew off the swing. She didn't want to lose her wing.

Annie liked swinging. She swung backwards and forwards.
She twizzled round and round. She swung high in the air.

WHEEEEEEE!

Annie saw Giraffe riding a bike.
She jumped off the swing.

"I want that bike," said Annie. "Give it to me."

"No," said Giraffe.

Annie opened her mouth with all her teeth sharp as swords.

SNIP-SNAP! went Annie's teeth, dangerously close to Giraffe's head.

Giraffe jumped off the bike.
He didn't want to lose his head.

Annie liked riding the bike. She rode into things
and over things and through things, and she SNIP,
SNIP-SNAPPED all over the place.

Everyone tried to jump out of the way.
Then they heard a noise.

TRAMP! **CRASH! TRAMP!**

Thud had arrived at the party.
"Now just behave," said her mother. "And don't go throwing your weight around. It's not nice."

Thud gave Monkey a big red balloon.
Monkey liked the balloon. She held it by
the string and ran with it.
    Annie jumped off the bike.

"I want that balloon," she said. "Give it to me."

"No," said Monkey, running away.

Annie opened her mouth with all her sharp, sharp teeth.

SNIP-SNAP! went Annie's teeth – and the balloon went ... BANG!

"That wasn't very nice," said Thud.
"Huh!" said Annie.

She opened her mouth
with all her sharp, sharp
teeth, dangerously close to
Thud's trunk. SNIP–

But Thud wrapped her trunk tightly round Annie's mouth.
She lifted Annie in the air and twirled her round –
ONE,
TWO,
THREE ...

WHEEEEEEEEE!

"Ooooh!" squealed Annie as she flew past the trees.
"Aaaargh!" she yelled as she whizzed over a swamp.
"Ow!" she shrieked as she fell into the river – SPLAT! –
right on top of her mother snoozing in the sun.

"Fancy you dropping in," said her mother. "You're back early. What happened?"

Annie sat in the dust on the river bank and cried real crocodile tears. "I got thrown out," she said.

"I see," said her mother. "Well, you know what you have to do." And she marched Annie back to the party.
"Annie has something to say," said her mother.
Annie hung her head. "Sorry," she whispered.
"Sorry, everyone. I'm very sorry, Monkey."
"Now just behave," said her mother.

Annie did. She played hide-and-seek, and hunt the bananas, and ring-a-ring o' roses. She had a lovely time – until the birthday cake came and everyone crowded round to see. Thud stood on Annie's tail – by mistake.

"Sorry," said Thud.
Annie opened her mouth with all her sharp, sharp teeth and ...

... SMILED!